Illustrations by Isabel Muñoz.

Written by Jane Kent.

Designed by Nick Ackland.

White Star Kids® is a registered trademark property of White Star s.r.l.

© 2019 White Star s.r.l.
Piazzale Luigi Cadorna, 6
20123 Milan, Italy
www.whitestar.it

Produced by i am a bookworm.

ISBN 978-88-544-1361-0
1 2 3 4 5 6   23 22 21 20 19

Printed in Turkey

The life of
Marie Curie

My name is Marie Curie and I am a Nobel Prize-winning physicist and chemist. During my life I made several groundbreaking scientific discoveries, including helping with the development of the X-ray and contributing to the fight against cancer.

Follow my story, from my humble beginnings in Poland to becoming a pioneer in the field of science.

I was born on 7th November, 1867, in the Polish city of Warsaw. My name is Maria Sklodowska, though I later used the name Marie instead. I was the youngest of five children - I had a brother called Józef and three sisters, Zosia, Bronya, and Hela.

Both of our parents were teachers. I excelled at school and took a particularly keen interest in Mathematics and Physics, the subjects taught by my father, Wladyslaw.

Józef

Bronya

Wladyslaw

In 1878 when I was just 10 years old, we lost my mother, Bronislawa, who died from tuberculosis. We began to struggle on my father's wage and so eventually I began to work as a governess. I continued to study Physics, Chemistry and Math in my spare time and dreamed about getting a degree, but I could not afford to pay for university and anyway, the University of Warsaw was men-only at that time.

However, my sister Bronya and I were able to strike up a deal. I would support her financially while she studied Medicine in Paris, and then she would do the same for me. So in 1891, filled with hope and excitement, I moved to France.

I began studying Physics and Math at Sorbonne University in Paris, completing my degree in Physics in 1893 and another degree in Math the next year. It was a tough time, as I had little money and survived mainly on bread and tea, but my appetite for learning got me through.

In 1894 I met Pierre Curie, a French physicist who was working in Paris. With our joint interest in science, we were perfect for each other. We married on 26th July the following year and went on to have two daughters - Irène was born in 1897 and Ève in 1904.

Marie

Pierre

Ève

Irène

My husband and I both became research workers at the School of Chemistry in 1896. We worked on separate projects, but gave each other help and advice. I was fascinated by the findings of another French physicist, Henri Becquerel, who had discovered that the element uranium casts off invisible rays able to pass through solid matter.

In 1897 I began to conduct my own experiments and found that, no matter what condition or form the uranium was in, the rays remained constant. My theory was that the rays came from the element's atomic structure and I described the phenomenon as "radioactivity". It was a revolutionary idea and lead to the creation of the field of atomic physics.

From then on, Pierre worked with me to further research radioactivity. In 1898 we began using the mineral pitchblende (uraninite), which contains uranium ore. We noticed that samples of pitchblende were a lot more radioactive than pure uranium and so we knew that there must be a tiny, tiny quantity of something else in there that nobody had ever found before. Although some scientists doubted our results, we believed we had found a new, unknown chemical element and set about proving it.

We began by grinding up samples of pitchblende, then dissolving them in acid and separating out all of the different elements. We succeeded in discovering a radioactive black powder within the pitchblende, which we named polonium after my home country of Poland. This new chemical element was given the symbol Po and atomic number 84.

Further investigation showed that the liquid left behind after we had extracted that polonium was still extremely radioactive. There was yet another new element present - in even smaller quantities, but with far more radioactivity! Now we needed to get a sample of it.

We called the new element radium and in late 1898 we published our evidence supporting its existence. However, we still had no sample. And to get one we needed a lot more pitchblende, which was expensive because it contains valuable uranium. Eventually I struck a deal with a factory in Austria that removed uranium from pitchblende to buy tonnes of the waste product, which was worthless to anyone but us. Then we set about extracting the tiny quantities of radium. We were working on a much larger scale than before, with much grinding, dissolving and filtering.

Not only was the work very physically demanding, there were also dangers that we did not yet know about. Our hands became red and sore, and we started to feel rather ill. While we put it down to simply being exhausted, it would later be revealed that our illness was an early symptom of radiation sickness.

We persevered and by 1902 we had finally produced a tiny - very tiny - quantity of pure radium. We had successfully proved the existence of this unique chemical element.

I earned my doctorate in Physics from the University of Paris in 1903. Later that same year, all of our hard work was rewarded when Pierre and I were presented with the Nobel Prize for Physics. Henri Becquerel won jointly with us, for his separate work on radioactivity. We used our award money to further our research and I would go down in history as the first woman to win a Nobel Prize.

My life was turned upside-down in 1906 when my beloved husband passed away, having been hit by a horse and cart. I knew he would want me to continue our research and so that is what I did. I also took over his position as Professor at Sorbonne, becoming the first female professor at the University, and picked up his lectures where he had left off.

I made history again in 1911 by winning a second Nobel Prize, this time in Chemistry for finding a way to measure radioactivity. I was the first person, man or woman, to win the award twice. Soon afterward, the first Radium Institute was built at Sorbonne. It had two laboratories - one was to be used for the study of radioactivity and the other to research the treatment of cancer.

The First World War began in 1914 and I wanted to do my bit to help. So I became the Director of the Red Cross Radiological Service and asked throughout Paris for money, supplies and vehicles that could be converted into mobile X-ray machines, small enough to take to the battlefront.

By October of that year, the first machines were ready and I set off for the battlefront with what became known as my "Petites Curies" ("Little Curies"). My 17-year-old daughter came with me and we worked together at casualty clearing stations to locate fractures, bullets and shrapnel in wounded men.

I used my fame to benefit my research, raising money to buy radium and to set up a radium research institute in Warsaw. I was also honored to have my name used by the Maric Curie Hospital in north London, which opened in 1930. As well as research facilities, it had women-only staff and used radiology to treat female cancer patients.

Sadly my life was cut short on 4th July, 1934, at 66 years old. I died from aplastic pernicious anaemia, which is believed to have been caused by prolonged exposure to radiation through my work with radioactive materials.

Many years later, in 1995, the French President François Mitterrand declared that Pierre and I be reburied together in the Panthéon. Only France's most important and admired dead are laid to rest at the mausoleum in Paris, and I was the first woman to be awarded a place in there.

A love of science runs in the Curie family. My eldest daughter, Irène, took after her parents and became a research scientist. She married Frédéric Joliot and they worked side-by-side on the nucleus of the atom, the center that contains protons and neutrons.

They discovered artificial radiation and, like Pierre and I, they were also awarded a Nobel Prize together. In 1956, Irène died of leukemia, another radiation-related illness. Hélène Langevin-Joliot, Irène's daughter and my granddaughter, also became a famous nuclear physicist.

If there's one thing I've learned in life, it's not to let anything hold you back, whether it be your gender, race, religion. Sadly, there will always be people who think that those who are different are somehow inferior. Prove them wrong! I am very glad to have helped people living with cancer, but also, hopefully, to have inspired more women to choose a career in the field of science.

She moved to France and began studying Physics and Math at Sorbonne University in Paris.

Curie was born on 7th November, in the Polish city of Warsaw.

Curie met a French physici... called Pierre.

1867   **1891**   **1894**

1878   **1893**

Curie earned a degree in Physics.

When Curie was just 10 years old, her mother died from tuberculosis.

They both became research workers at the School of Chemistry.

Using the mineral pitchblende, they found two new chemical elements - a radioactive black powder called polonium and radium, which they had no sample of.

1896

1898

1895

1897

1902

Their daughter Irène was born. Following the work of physicist Henri Becquerel, Curie began to conduct her own experiments and discovered radioactivity.

They produced a tiny quantity of pure radium.

Pierre and Curie married.

The Curies won the Nobel Prize for Physics, jointly with Henri Becquerel. Curie was the first woman to do so.

She created mobile X-rays called "Petites Curies" and took them to the battlefront of First World War.

Pierre died in a street accident. Curie took over his job and became the first female Professor at Sorbonne University.

1903

1906

1914

1904

1911

Their daughter Ève was born.

Curie won a second Nobel Prize for Chemistry. She was the first person to win two Nobel Prizes. The first Radium Institute was built at Sorbonne.

Curie died at 66 years old from aplastic pernicious anaemia, caused by prolonged exposure to radiation.

The French President ordered that the Curies be reburied together in the Panthéon.

1934

1995

1930

1944

The Marie Curie Hospital was opened in north London.

A bomb almost entirely destroyed the Marie Curie Hospital.

QUESTIONS

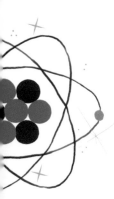

Q1. Where was Marie Curie born?

Q2. In what year did she move to France?

Q3. What were Curie's two degree subjects?

Q4. What was the name of Curie's husband?

Q5. What did the Curies name
the radioactive black powder
they discovered?

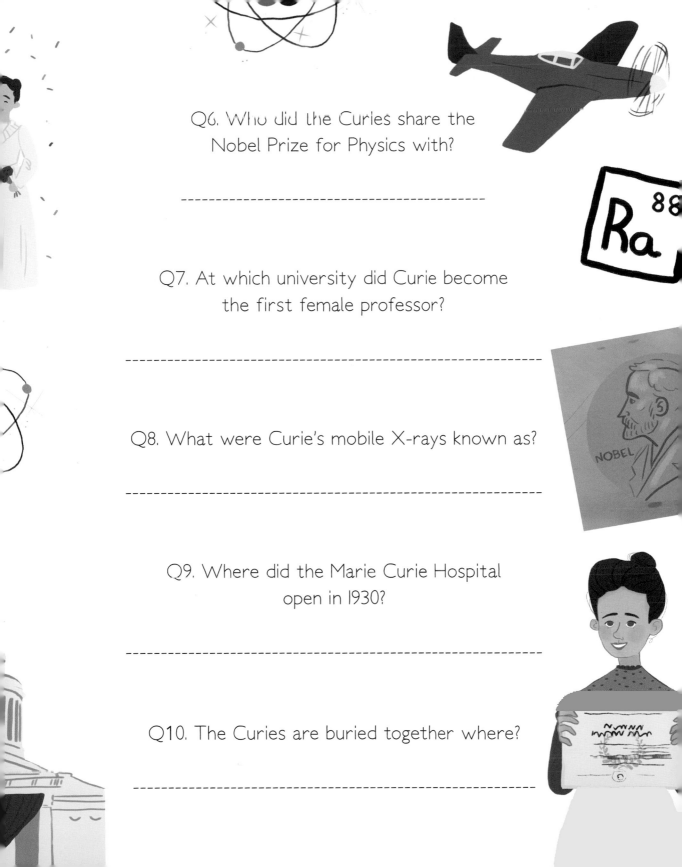

Q6. Who did the Curies share the Nobel Prize for Physics with?

Q7. At which university did Curie become the first female professor?

Q8. What were Curie's mobile X-rays known as?

Q9. Where did the Marie Curie Hospital open in 1930?

Q10. The Curies are buried together where?

ANSWERS

A1. Warsaw, Poland.

A2. 1891.

A3. Physics and Mathematics.

A4. Pierre.

A5. Polonium, after her home country of Poland.

A6. Henri Becquerel.

A7. Sorbonne University.

A8. "Petites Curies" ("Little Curies").

A9. North London.

A10. The Panthéon.